CUMBRIA LIBRARIES

KT-178-117

3 8003 04839 7921

HAVE YOU READ THESE
SPY TOYS ADVENTURES?

spytoysbooks.com

SPY TOYS
UNDERCOVER

MARK POWERS

ILLUSTRATED BY
TIM WESSON

BLOOMSBURY

LONDON OXFORD NEW YORK NEW DELHI SYDNEY

Bloomsbury Publishing, London, Oxford, New York, New Delhi and Sydney

First published in Great Britain in February 2018 by Bloomsbury Publishing Plc
50 Bedford Square, London WC1B 3DP

www.bloomsbury.com

BLOOMSBURY is a registered trademark of Bloomsbury Publishing Plc

Text copyright © Mark Griffiths 2018
Illustrations copyright © Tim Wesson 2018

The moral rights of the author and illustrator have been asserted

All rights reserved
No part of this publication may be reproduced or
transmitted by any means, electronic, mechanical, photocopying or
otherwise, without the prior permission of the publisher

A CIP catalogue record for this book is available from the British Library

ISBN 978 1 4088 7090 7

Printed and bound in Great Britain by CPI Group (UK) Ltd, Croydon CR0 4YY

1 3 5 7 9 10 8 6 4 2

For Leanne

With thanks to Jo, Kate, Tim,
Zöe, Hannah, Lizz, Charlotte
and all at Bloomsbury

CHAPTER ONE

ARTHUR PARKINSON
GETS A SURPRISE

The old man hurrying along the deserted street was about to have the strangest day of his life.

It was a smidgen before six o'clock on a chilly March morning. A Monday. At this hour most people are snoozing restlessly under their duvets, trying not to think about the coming week at work or school, but the old man didn't mind being up this early. He was whistling a tune to himself as he walked briskly along, thinking about how lucky he was to work in a chocolate factory.

Arthur Parkinson had been caretaker at the Chimpwick's Chocolate manufacturing plant for twenty-nine years. The hours suited him, his co-workers were friendly and the factory was just a short walk from his house. He even liked that he always came home smelling of chocolate. There are worse things for a person to smell of – as his  friend Haddocky Brian, who worked in the fishmonger's, often complained.

This morning Arthur Parkinson was in a

particularly good mood because he had a new torch. This may not sound like a big deal, but Arthur felt like a medieval knight with a brand new sword who was just itching for a bit of stabby, dragon-slaying action to break it in. One of Arthur's main duties at the factory was fixing things. Not the big, chocolate-producing machines – they were fixed automatically by robots – but the little things: stopped taps, grumbling radiators, popped light bulbs. These were the times you needed a sturdy, reliable torch at hand; and having one always made Arthur feel he could solve any problem. He switched the torch on and marvelled at the way its powerful whitish-yellow beam stretched far off into the morning gloom like a long finger of light.

He nodded to himself, pleased. As torches went, this really was a cracker. He switched it off and stowed it securely in his coat pocket.

Above the rooftops of the town, the sky was slowly turning pink, the sun readying itself to peep over the horizon and mark the beginning of another day.

Nearing the old wrought-iron factory gates, Arthur took out a weighty bunch of keys. He opened the large iron lock and pushed open one of the gates. As it swung open, it made the same satisfying creak it had made for the past twenty-nine years. Then Arthur stopped, frozen to the spot, his mouth slowly sagging open.

He shook his head. What he was seeing – or rather, what he was *not* seeing – was ridiculous. *Snap out of it, Arthur,* he told himself. *Get a grip.* Heart racing, he dug in his pocket for his new torch, switched it to its brightest setting and swung the beam before him in a slow, steady arc ... But there was nothing to see. The entire Chimpwick's Chocolate factory had disappeared.

CHAPTER TWO

PANDORA GREBE GETS IN A SPIN

If you ever take a sightseeing tour of London, the bus is unlikely to go down Mulbarton Street. It's a dull road. There's an estate agent's. A not-very-good sandwich bar. Several old, grey houses. A scrubby little park enclosed by rusty iron railings. A ramshackle old toyshop. Nothing to get excited about.

Or so you might think.

What the tour guides don't know is that the ramshackle old toyshop in Mulbarton

Street is actually a disguise. Any tour guide worth their salt would be thrilled to learn that behind the grimy shopfront lies the secret entrance to the headquarters of Spy Toys, the most astounding team of secret agents in the whole **DEPARTMENT OF SECRET AFFAIRS** – three robotic toy rejects far too dangerous to be children's playthings, and who now spend their days fighting crime.

In the luxurious apartment hidden behind the Mulbarton Street toyshop, the three Spy Toys – Dan the teddy bear, Arabella the rag doll and Flax the rabbit – were lounging in comfortable chairs while an excitable young woman in a sharp business suit perched on a stool between them. She was clutching a notebook and pen.

'Such a pleasure to meet you, guys!' enthused the woman, whose name was Pandora Grebe. She had a posh, drawling voice that made her sound a bit like a sleepy cat. 'I'm so looking forward to hearing all about your crazy adventures! The readers of **SPIES & SPYING MONTHLY** are going to be *thrilled*, I just know. Let me see if my research is correct.' She stabbed her pen in Dan's direction. 'Dan, you're a Snugaliffic Cuddlestar teddy bear. Due to a manufacturing error at the Snaztacular Ultrafun toy factory where you were made, you have super-strength, yes?'

Dan smiled modestly, picked up an iron bar lying next to his chair and bent it into a heart shape, which he then presented to Pandora. 'Yes, Pandora,' he said. 'Yes, I have.'

Pandora beamed. 'Gosh! that's *a*-mazing!'

Arabella the rag doll rolled her eyes. 'Now I know why he bought that iron bar this morning. What a show-off.'

Pandora laughed and turned to her. 'And

you, *sweetie*! Arabella the Loadsasmiles Sunshine Rag Doll. A fault in your manufacture left you rather too ... *grumpy*, shall we say, to be a child's toy. But what you lack in kid-friendliness you make up for in kick-butt fighting skills. Is that right?'

'It's all peachy except the bit where you called me "sweetie",' said Arabella. 'No one

calls me "sweetie". Not unless they're looking for trouble.' She winked at Pandora. 'You with me, *sweetie*?'

Pandora swiftly erased something on her pad with the end of her pencil. 'Absolutely, *swee*– er, I mean Arabella.' She turned hurriedly to the small white rabbit. 'And lastly we have Flax. Not actually a toy at all, I understand, but an ex-police robot made in the shape of a rabbit. You're the technical whizz, I believe? Good with gadgets and so on?'

Flax nodded and fiddled with his tie. 'I do possess certain skills. One of which is *research*, and do you know –' and here he narrowed his small pink eyes at Pandora – 'I cannot find a single reference to your

SPIES & SPYING MONTHLY anywhere? It's almost as if the magazine doesn't exist.'

'Funny, that,' agreed Dan.

'Yeah,' said Arabella. 'And what would be the purpose of it anyway? The whole point of spying is to keep it secret. Not blab about it in magazines.'

Pandora gulped and dropped her notepad. 'I – I can explain!' she stammered. '**SPIES & SPYING MONTHLY** is brand new. We're still putting together the first issue. And it's only going to be available to government staff with full security clearance. It's perfectly safe to speak to me! Honestly!'

'And do you know another thing?' continued Flax. 'In all my research I couldn't find a single reference anywhere to a person called Pandora Grebe. It's like you simply made the name up!'

'Isn't that strange?' said Dan with a smirk.

'It's my pen name!' insisted Pandora. 'My real name is Anne Snib, but that sounded boring so I changed it.'

'You're not a journalist at all,' said Flax. 'You're a spy. Sent here by some enemy to get info on us.'

'Looks like you've been found out,' Arabella said, with a grin. 'Sweetie.'

'I thought you'd like being in the magazine!' protested Pandora. 'I was doing you a good turn!'

'Forgive the pun,' said Flax, 'but I think you'll find one good turn deserves another.'

Pandora frowned. 'What pun?'

'This one,' said Flax, and he pressed a button on a control panel built into the armrest of his chair. The stool on which Pandora was sitting began to spin around, slowly at first and then with increasing speed.

Pandora squeaked in alarm and clung desperately to the edge of the stool. 'W-w-what's going on?'

Flax consulted his watch. 'Time to open the skylight. Dan, would you?'

Dan pulled a long cord, and a large square skylight in the ceiling slid open.

Flax touched another control on his armrest. Pandora's revolving stool began to rise, its single central leg extending until it carried her up through the skylight and out into the nippy morning air.

'Help!' cried the hapless young woman on the spinning stool. She looked like she was riding the world's smallest and least fun roundabout. 'You're making me giddy!'

Flax checked his watch again. 'Four ...

three … two … one!' He gave a dial on his armrest a sharp twist and the spinning stool's speed increased tenfold. Pandora Grebe flew off it, fast as a meteor.

Screaming, she sailed gracefully through the sky and began to plummet towards the squat form of a rubbish barge pootling its way across the Thames. The little boat was piled with stinking household refuse. The three Spy Toys watched as Pandora Grebe headed for the barge at high speed – and then missed it, plunging into the grey waters of the Thames with a quiet *splish*. After a second, she bobbed to the surface looking thoroughly miffed and sopping wet. A seagull flew down and landed on her head. She batted it away angrily.

'*Oops*,' said Dan mildly. 'Just missed, Flax.'

The rabbit shrugged. 'Still works for me. What I want to know is how a spy managed to find out all that information about us. Maybe there's been some kind of data security breach?' He scurried over to a computer and began bashing away at the keyboard.

'Relax, cottontail!' said Arabella. 'We got rid of her, didn't we?'

Flax snorted. 'Relax? How can any of us relax? The whole **DEPARTMENT OF SECRET AFFAIRS** might be leaking information to enemy powers as we speak.'

Dan shook his head at Arabella. 'Does that rabbit ever switch off? It's OK to take a break sometimes, you know.'

Suddenly an alarm blared and a huge TV screen began to lower itself from the ceiling of the living room.

'That'll be Auntie Roz with a new mission for us!' said Arabella. They rushed to the screen. Auntie Roz was the head of the Department of Secret Affairs.

A woman's face appeared. It was a large, powerful face with large features, topped off with a large amount of yellow hair. It was the sort of face that looked like it might be very frightening when it was angry. Fortunately, for the moment it was smiling.

'Team!' said Auntie Roz briskly (she was a busy woman with no time to waste on pleasantries. At home, she employed a servant whose sole job was to say 'nighty-night' to her children every evening). 'Have you heard of Chimpwick's Chocolate?'

'Of course,' said Flax. 'They have that TV

advert with the singing cartoon chimpanzee: *Chimpwick's Chocolate Makes Your Taste Buds Burst, All Other Chocolate in the World Is the Worst.* A crude but effective little ditty.'

Arabella groaned. 'Thanks, big ears! I've been trying to get that awful song out of my head for weeks.'

Auntie Roz nodded. 'Chimpwick's is the number one brand of chocolate in the world. Children are obsessed with the stuff. Which is about to become a massive problem.' There was a click, and an image of a huge black hole in the ground surrounded by a chain-link fence appeared on the screen. 'Last night the entire Chimpwick's Chocolate factory vanished. Into, as they say, *thin air*. Can you imagine what'll happen when news of this gets out? Kids will go crazy without their Chimpwick's Chocolate. If that factory isn't found soon there'll be panic, rioting – chaos on a grand scale.'

'So who do we think's responsible?' asked Arabella. 'Crack squad of guerrilla dentists? Billionaire sprout farmer with a grudge?

Thirty-storey diabetic lizard monster?'

'Our best guess so far,' said Auntie Roz, 'is *this* woman.' A photo appeared of a stern-faced woman in her thirties with dark-rimmed glasses and a long ponytail. 'Her name is Paula Dimpling.'

'*She* removed an entire chocolate factory?' asked Dan. 'Are you sure? She doesn't look like she has the upper-body strength.'

'She's a scientist,' said Auntie Roz. 'A total, certified genius. Used to work at the chocolate factory inventing new products. The salted-caramel starfish was one of hers.

STARFISH

SALTED CARAMEL

'Our sources say she recently walked out in a huff. Had a big argument with the boss. Now she teaches science at a nearby primary school.

'We reckon if anyone has the motive and the intelligence to make an entire chocolate factory vanish, it's her.'

Flax shrugged. 'So go over there and slap a pair of handcuffs on her.'

'Ha!' said Auntie Roz. 'First, we need proof. We need to get close to her, find out if she's really involved. And by *we*, I do of course mean *you*. You will go undercover into the school where she teaches and investigate.'

Arabella folded her arms. 'Oh, terrific! Stuck in some smelly old class toy box all day, getting mauled by a bunch of sticky-fingered brats. Just what I always wanted!'

Auntie Roz smiled an odd, knowing smile. 'That's not quite what I meant by undercover. Meet me at the **DEPARTMENT OF SECRET AFFAIRS**, Tech Division, in one hour.'

'Sounds intriguing,' said Flax. 'We'll be there.'

'Oh – one last thing,' said Auntie Roz.

The three Spy Toys looked at her expectantly.

'An ex-colleague of mine is coming to see you today. Goes by the name of Pandora Grebe. She wants to profile you for a brand new magazine we're helping set up, **SPIES & SPYING MONTHLY**. Exciting, eh?'

Dan, Arabella and Flax exchanged a swift look.

'Sounds great,' said Flax. 'We'll keep an eye out for her.'

Sixty minutes later, Dan, Flax and Arabella were sitting in the reception area of the Tech Division of the **DEPARTMENT OF SECRET AFFAIRS**. It was a smallish room with a row of seats, a shiny vending machine and a desk, behind which sat a bored young woman playing a game on her mobile phone. The phone was making a lot of loud beeping and exploding noises.

The door opened and Auntie Roz bustled in, bristling with energy. 'Ah, good. You're here. Welcome to Tech Division. Shall we get started? I want you to meet our tech expert, Dr Willows.'

'Lead the way!' said Flax eagerly, ever the gadget buff. 'Are they in the main building?'

Auntie Roz looked puzzled. 'I don't understand. This IS the main building. This is the whole department.'

'This one little room?' said Flax. 'I thought this was just the reception area!'

'See that?' said Auntie Roz, pointing at the vending machine. 'That is the very latest 3D SwiftoPrint. It can manufacture any piece of technology you need almost instantly, simply by being fed the required

27

specifications. We don't need huge expensive labs any more.'

Flax laughed delightedly. 'Impressive! And who invented that?'

'I did,' said the young woman behind the desk. She was still staring at the screen of her phone, intent on her game. 'Erm ... hang on a sec,' she muttered. There was a loud electronic crashing noise from the phone and a brief musical fanfare. 'Darn it! Five

points away from my highest ever score.' She stood up. 'Anyway – hiya, I'm Dr Willows. Just give me a moment to scan you guys.' She pointed her mobile phone at Flax, Arabella and Dan in turn. Each time the phone emitted a loud **BEEEEEEEP**.

'So what the heck's going on here?' asked Arabella. 'How's this lady gonna help us go undercover in a school? A place, incidentally, I am not looking forward to visiting. Did I ever tell you guys how much I hate kids?'

'Yeah,' said Dan. 'Quite often. And in some detail.'

'You won't be going undercover as toys,' said Auntie Roz. 'You'll be going undercover as *children*.'

Arabella spluttered. 'How? Gonna take

more than a few make-up tips to make furball here pass for a schoolkid.'

'Then check this out,' said Dr Willows, and pointed her phone at the 3D SwiftoPrint. There was a different, louder **BEEEEEP** noise and the machine began to whir and hum.

'I believe your new outfits are cooking now,' said Auntie Roz.

The machine pinged like a microwave oven and dispensed three neat, flat, square packages, each about the size of a CD. Auntie Roz handed one apiece to the Spy Toys. 'Dr Willows – if you would kindly explain?'

'Yeah, for sure,' said Dr Willows. 'Maybe it'll be easier if I show rather than tell? On each of your packages you will see a small red button. Please press that button now.'

Flax, Arabella and Dan pressed their buttons. There was a noise like crackling electricity and the three packages suddenly sprang open with an intense flash of blue light. The three Spy Toys staggered and rubbed their eyes.

'What happened?' asked Flax blearily.

'Your face!' Arabella gasped at Dan.

'*Your face*!' Dan gasped at Arabella.

'*My* face!' cried Flax, looking at his reflection in the shiny surface of the 3D SwiftoPrint machine. He motioned for Dan and Arabella to join him.

The rabbit, the rag doll and the teddy bear stared at their reflections.

The three children staring back at them looked to be around ten years of age. Where Dan had stood, there was now a stocky boy with a spray of untidy red hair and a confused expression. In Arabella's place slouched a gloomy-looking girl with long raven-black tresses. And staring back at Flax was a skinny fair-haired boy wearing thick-lensed glasses. All three were wearing the same slightly grubby dark green school uniform.

The toys tried to speak but were too astonished to utter a sound.

'Nifty, eh?' said Dr Willows with a touch of pride. 'The very latest thing in *android bodysuits*. A complete robotic outer skin to create the perfect disguise. Totally realistic. Totally undetectable.'

Flax examined his reflection. He pulled a series of funny faces and found the boy's face in his reflection mirroring his expressions in a completely lifelike and convincing way. It was astonishing, as if a second, human skin had sprouted from his own. Then he noticed his glasses were held together with a sticking plaster. 'Blimey,' he muttered softly. 'I'm a nerd.'

Arabella snorted. 'Like that's a surprise.'

'If you feel the top of your heads,' said Dr Willows, 'there's a small round button just under your hair. Press that when your mission's over and the bodysuit will automatically remove itself.' She picked up her phone and began playing her game again.

Flax fingered his scalp gingerly. Under his mop of fair hair, he could make out a firm round shape about the size of a pound coin. 'This will take a little getting used to,' he muttered. 'When do we start investigating?'

'Good question!' said Auntie Roz, beaming. 'Better get some rest, you three. School in the morning!'

CHAPTER THREE

SUITS ME

Water Shrew Lane Primary was a small school situated only a few streets away from the site of the missing Chimpwick's Chocolate factory. It was early on a Tuesday morning and several children were hanging around in the playground, chatting and laughing before the school day began.

At 8:45 Auntie Roz dropped off Flax, Arabella and Dan in their disguises at the school gate. Auntie Roz herself was dressed in the T-shirt, tracksuit bottoms and dressing gown of a busy parent doing the school run.

As they stepped from the scuffed and dented car she had selected specially for the mission, she gave her secret agents a motherly wave. 'Enjoy your first day, my little darlings! I hope you learn lots of interesting stuff!' And with that she honked the horn and the car roared away.

The three Spy Toys trudged slowly towards the main entrance of the school, aware that all heads in the playground were swivelling to check out Water Shrew Lane Primary's three newest pupils.

'*Yeuch,*' grumbled Arabella. '*Kids.* If any of them come near me, I'm going to flatten them. *Pow!* Just like that.'

'Easy now,' murmured Flax. 'Let's try not to attract attention. We're here to do a job.'

'I know,' muttered Arabella, 'but do you have to suck the fun out of everything?'

Dan was silent and glum. Arabella nudged him. 'What's your problem, furball? Not scared of a few ankle-biters, are you?'

Dan shook his head. 'No. But I was built for hugging and fun. Not to sit in a classroom all day learning things. What if I can't do the work?'

Arabella shrugged. 'Maybe there's a football team you can try out for. I'm sure they wouldn't turn down a striker who can kick the ball harder than a rhinoceros.'

'Good morning, class.'

'Good mor-ning, Miss-us Dimp-ling.'

Mrs Dimpling removed her glasses, breathed on them, polished them on the hem of her jumper and then replaced them on her nose. Behind their lenses, her two small eyes darted like tiny fish in an aquarium. Then she took a gulp from a mug of steaming coffee and consulted a small slip of paper. 'In his wisdom, the head teacher has dumped three more children into our already-overstretched class. The new pupils are called Arabella, Dan and –' she squinted at the paper – '*Flax*, is that? I can never keep up with these trendy new names. Oh well. Say hello to them, class.'

She motioned at the newcomers with a bored hand while she drained the last of her coffee.

'*Hell-o, Ar-a-bell-a. Hell-o, Dan. Hell-o, Flax*,' chorused the class.

Arabella spun around in her chair, grinning, arms wide, as if challenging the whole class to a fight. Dan and Flax both turned and waved shyly at the other children.

Mrs Dimpling directed her gaze at the three new pupils. 'Now listen, you three. Let's get this straight from the start. There's no messing about in my class. No gossiping, giggling or gallivanting. I want no crying, carping, fussing or fretting. I'm not your mother or your babysitter. I'm not your friend. I'm here to teach and you're here to shut up and listen. Got it?'

Without waiting for a response, she plonked a plastic container full of pencils on the desk in front of Arabella.

'You, lady. Stop daydreaming about butterflies and ponies. Give these out. In silence. One each. And then give me back the box.'

Flax and Dan both winced. They had never known anyone to speak like this to Arabella before.

'And I know how many are in there, in case you're thinking of pinching any,' continued Mrs Dimpling.

Arabella was out of her seat before Flax or Dan could stop her. She picked up the box of pencils and with all her strength threw it at the floor, where it shattered with a bang, scattering pencils in all directions.

The class let out a gasp.

Mrs Dimpling spun around, tiny eyes blazing behind her thick glasses.

Flax and Dan put their heads in their hands.

'Now *you* listen here, missy,' growled Arabella. 'I might be as mean as a scorpion who's just stubbed her toe, but one thing I am *not* is a *thief*! Got that?'

An icy silence descended on the class. No one dared breathe. Mrs Dimpling's fingers tightened around her pen. She took a deep breath and adjusted her glasses. 'Please wait in the corridor, Arabella,' she said in a quiet voice that sounded like the first gentle rumbles a volcano makes before it blows its top. 'I'll deal with you later.'

'Suits me,' retorted Arabella, and she

stalked from the room, kicking the spilt pencils out of her way and sending them skittering along the floor.

'Jack!' called Mrs Dimpling. 'Clean up this mess. Quick as you like.'

A small terrier-like boy with wiry hair sprang from his seat and began to scoop up the pencils.

'Now,' said Mrs Dimpling, turning back to her board, 'ahead of Friday's trip to the **WORLDLAND MODEL VILLAGE**, where they recreate great cities in miniature, we'll continue with our project on capitals of the world. Take out your capital cities worksheets, please.'

The class began rummaging in bags.

Dan raised a nervous hand. 'Miss? Miss?'

Mrs Dimpling glared at him. 'What now, boy?'

Dan's words came out in one long gabble. 'Miss, we're new and we don't have worksheets because we're new, and we can't do the work because we're new, and we haven't got any worksheets so we can't do the work, and we haven't got any worksheets ... ?'

Mrs Dimpling rolled her eyes. 'Fine, fine. Wait a minute.'

She stumped to the back of the classroom, unlocked a door leading to a small storeroom and went in.

Flax raised his eyebrows at Dan. 'Look at how she keeps that place locked up,' he whispered. 'If she's hiding anything suspicious, I bet it's in there.'

'What might she be hiding?'

Flax shrugged. 'Plans for a giant crane that can lift an entire factory? Or some kind of shrinking ray, maybe? Who knows? But we're going to find out.'

Dan tugged at the sleeve of his pullover nervously. 'What do we do if she hasn't got any worksheets?'

Flax groaned. 'You need to calm down, Dan. Seriously. We're here to carry out a mission. That's all. You're not really a schoolkid.'

A few moments later, Mrs Dimpling emerged from the storeroom brandishing two spare worksheets. She handed them one each. Dan let out a sigh of relief.

'Right,' said Mrs Dimpling. 'Today we'll

look at European capitals. Let's start with France. Who can tell me its capital city? As a clue I can tell you it's famous for having a very tall tower.'

The class let out a burst of laughter.

'Did I say something *funny*?' asked Mrs Dimpling. Her tone made it very clear what answer she expected.

To her amazement, the class erupted in laughter again.

'What's going on?' she demanded.

The boy called Jack pointed at the classroom door with a look of disbelief. Frowning, Mrs Dimpling turned and saw Arabella with her nose squished up, piglike, against the window, pulling funny faces.

When the lesson ended, Dan, Flax and the other children pulled on their coats and filed out into the playground for morning break. On their way out they passed Arabella, who was leaning against the wall with her arms folded, doing her best to look bored. 'Oh, great,' she said, seeing them, her mood brightening. 'Playtime. Cool!'

'Not you, Arabella,' called Mrs Dimpling's voice from the classroom. 'Come here. I want a word.'

'Oh, what now?' groaned Arabella, and trudged back into the classroom.

Outside it was a bright, cold morning. A few small white clouds trundled across the blueness of the sky. Flax and Dan peered through the window into their classroom, where Mrs Dimpling sat at her desk giving a lengthy lecture to a stroppy-looking Arabella.

'Not quite mastered this blending-in business, has she?' remarked Flax.

Dan shrugged. 'I guess a naughty pupil is just as good a disguise as a well-behaved one.'

'I was hoping Mrs D would nip off to the staffroom or wherever it is that teachers go at breaktime,' said Flax. 'Then we could search her storeroom. Maybe we can do that at lunch? In the meantime, let's split up. Speak to the pupils. Maybe someone's noticed her acting suspiciously.'

Dan sauntered through the playground, looking for someone to speak to. Most children were playing together in small groups, kicking balls and chasing one another, laughing and screaming with delight. Despite Flax's reminder that they were here purely to gather information, Dan couldn't help wanting to join in with the games, half hoping one of the boys playing football would run up to him and say they were a man short in their five-a-side match. Then, suddenly, he heard the sound of someone crying. In the corner of the playground, near a climbing frame, he noticed a small girl with frizzy hair pleading desperately with a tall, heavily built boy, who was holding a fluffy brown school bag above his head and cackling.

A hand tapped the boy on the shoulder. He swung around to find a squat, red-haired boy facing him. 'Hi!' said Dan brightly. 'You'll be returning this girl's property now. Right now. Understand?'

The tall boy laughed splutteringly. 'Oh yeah?' He jabbed a finger at Dan's chest. 'And you're going to stop me, are you? Little boy?' He squared up to Dan, trying to make himself look as big and threatening as possible.

'Please don't,' the frizzy-haired girl hissed at Dan. 'You'll only make things worse.'

'No,' laughed the tall boy, 'please do. I could do with a giggle.' He jabbed Dan in the chest again. 'Go on. Little boy. I –'

He had meant to say 'I dare you', but when Dan suddenly pulled the climbing frame out of the ground and twisted it around the tall boy, forming a tiny metal cage, trapping him firmly inside it, he forgot how his sentence was supposed to end. 'Whhhaaaaaaaaaaaaaaaa?' he said instead, peering out meekly through the bars.

Dan plucked the girl's bag from the boy's hands.

Smiling, he leaned down and whispered in the boy's ear, 'You ever steal anything

from this girl again – or try any nasty foolishness to get your own back – and the next thing I bend out of shape won't be this climbing frame. You with me, pal?'

The tall boy nodded dumbly. 'Yes,' he mumbled. 'Yes, sir.'

With astounding speed, Dan quickly unbent the climbing frame and replaced it in the ground where it had previously stood. He'd been so quick that no one else in the playground had noticed the climbing frame vanish and reappear again. The tall boy blinked and wandered away on unsteady legs.

Dan handed the furry brown bag back to the girl, noticing with a small smile that it was shaped like a teddy bear. The little girl hugged the bag to her.

'Thank you!' she cried. 'That was amazing! I owe you a big favour. If you ever need anything, just ask.'

'Actually,' said Dan. 'There is something.'

'Yes?'

He drew a crumpled worksheet from his pocket. 'I'm still having trouble remembering all these capital cities. Can you test me?'

At the rear of the playground, Flax noticed a rickety wooden building resembling a large garden shed. There was a sign taped to its door saying **SCIENCE CLUB**. He peered through its window. A small group of boys and girls were fussing around some object laid out on a long table, poking and prodding at it with screwdrivers and other tools. Flax recognised one of the boys as Jack, the wiry-haired kid whom Mrs Dimpling had ordered to pick up the pencils. The boy dropped his screwdriver, and as he bent to retrieve it, Flax finally got a good look at the object on the table. It was an odd furry creature about the size of a dog, with a short stubby snout and extremely long limbs that ended in hook-like claws. A panel in its head was open, revealing a mass of electronic circuits. Flax pushed open the door of the shed. The children looked up at him with wide, wary eyes. 'Nice robotic sloth!' he said in a friendly voice.

Jack smiled. 'Thanks. It's a Snaztacular Ultrafun Sleepytime Sloth. A friend asked us to make some modifications to her favourite cuddly toy. Thinks he's too soppy! It's our project. Mum lets us work on him at breaktimes.'

'Your mum?'

'Mrs Dimpling,' said Jack.

Flax shuddered. *Tough break, kid*, he thought. But then he realised Jack could be a valuable source of information for the mission. He examined the motionless form of the sloth with interest. 'So what are these modifications?'

'Replacing his flimsy metal skeleton with a mega-tough plastic one. Adding extra-sharp teeth. Souping up his personality program to heighten his aggression.' Jack chuckled. 'Basically, our friend wants us to make him into the baddest sloth you ever saw!'

'Wow! That's really advanced stuff! You lot must be geniuses!'

The children blushed modestly but did not contradict him.

Flax took a screwdriver from the table and poked it gingerly into the complicated electronics visible within the robotic sloth's skull. He bent down and peered inside. 'I reckon that if you wire the emotion chip directly to the mouth control, you could increase his aggression by over seventy-five per cent.'

Jack's eyes widened. 'Cool idea! You know about robots, do you?'

Flax gave a shrug. 'Teeny bit.'

Carefully, he removed several wires from tiny sockets in the sloth's head and plugged them into new locations. Then he flicked the **POWER ON** switch located just behind the sloth's right ear. Immediately, the sloth let out a blood-curdling roar that would have given a tiger the heebie-jeebies.

Flax quickly flicked the switch behind the sloth's ear to **POWER ON** but it had no effect, and the angry sloth suddenly leaped off the table and began advancing on the children, growling like a fierce dog. Someone screamed.

'Oops,' said Flax. 'Think I accidentally overrode the power coupling. No problem.' He rummaged in his school bag and drew out a device that looked a little like a stubby torch. He pointed it at the snarling sloth. There was a loud buzzing noise and the mechanical sloth suddenly fell silent and froze.

The children gasped with relief.

'It's an EMP emitter,' explained Flax, brandishing the device. 'Sends out a sharp burst of energy that interferes with electronic circuits. Very handy for stopping runaway technology.'

Jack stared at the device in wonder. 'I thought only the government had access to technology like that! Where did you get it?'

Flax hesitated for a second and then shrugged. 'Car boot sale. Amazing what you can pick up if you get there early.'

The bell rang, signalling the end of break. When Dan and Flax re-entered the classroom they found Arabella sitting in her seat, quietly filling in a worksheet. Flax tapped her arm.

'I've made an important contact,' he whispered. 'The boy Jack is Mrs Dimpling's son. I reckon I can get plenty of good information about his mother out of him.'

Arabella waved a dismissive hand. 'I've been chinwagging with the lady herself at breaktime. Turns out the old battleaxe ain't so bad when you get to know her. She hates kids, too! She told me *everything*.'

'Great going!' said Dan, impressed. 'So what's the story, then? Is she involved in the disappearance of the chocolate factory?'

The rag doll shook her head. 'She ain't involved at all. She told me she left the chocolate factory because they wanted everyone working there to dress like elves to make it seem magical. How embarrassing is that? She hated the idea, of course, so she quit, and this was the only job she's been able to get in the meantime because she has such lousy people skills. She's no fan of the bosses at Chimpwick's, but she loves the chocolate itself and the idea of the world running out of it makes her mighty itchy. So it looks like coming to this dump full of brats has been a complete waste of time.'

The frizzy-haired girl whose bag Dan had returned came into the classroom and gave him a beaming smile as she passed their table.

'Oh, I don't know,' said Dan.

The school day wore on. At lunchtime, Flax wanted to discuss some new theories he had about the missing chocolate factory, but Dan and Arabella just rolled their eyes, called him a 'boring bunny' and ran off to play with the other children, much to his annoyance. In the afternoon, their class had a PE lesson. Dan thought this might be his chance to impress his classmates with his super-strength, but unfortunately neither he, Arabella nor Flax had brought any PE kit with them, so they had to spend the lesson sitting on a wooden bench watching the other kids have a good time playing rugby.

Jack Dimpling had also forgotten his PE kit. He was sitting next to Flax on the bench, staring at the screen of his smartphone, his brow furrowed in concentration.

'You making an early start on our maths homework?' asked Flax.

Jack laughed lightly. 'Ah, no. I'm playing

TURBO BADGER. It's the coolest game ever. You want a go?'

Flax shook his head. 'I don't do games. Waste of time.'

'Not this one,' said Jack. 'It's brilliant.' He passed the smartphone to Flax. 'You're a badger flying over Saladville in your turbocopter, see? And you have to zap the cabbages with your laser zonker as they zoom past. You press this button here to fire. Go on. Try it! I'll restart the game for you ...'

'Must I?' said Flax irritably, but then, realising he probably shouldn't appear rude, he looked down at the screen of Jack's smartphone as the game reset itself and fresh batches of animated cabbages began to streak past the helicopter at the bottom of the screen.

'Now!' said Jack. 'Fire!'

Flax jabbed the fire button rapidly. On the screen, a red laser bolt zapped from a cannon on the front of the helicopter and blew up several of the cabbages. The game played a happy little fanfare sound.

'Nice shooting!' said Jack. 'That last one was a Boss Cabbage worth five hundred points!'

Flax shrugged. 'And that's good, is it?'

'It's great! I've never been able to hit one and I've been playing this game for weeks. You must have superhuman reactions!'

Flax shrugged modestly. 'Oh, maybe just a little. Oh look! I've hit another one!' He gave a little chuckle of pleasure.

Jack shook his head in wonder. 'Wow! You're a **TURBO BADGER** natural!'

There was a **TUMP** sound and the PE class's rugby ball suddenly dropped at Dan's feet.

'Throw it back, please!' called one of the kids on the pitch.

Dan picked up the ball and prepared to throw it – only to have Arabella snatch it from his grip.

'I got this, fluffbrain,' she drawled. 'You'd only chuck it into the next county or something and attract attention. We have to play nice with these kiddiewinks, remember?'

Dan gave a sheepish nod. 'I understand.'

'OK, then.' She threw the ball at the kid with all her might. It struck him squarely on the forehead and he collapsed with a groan.

Arabella cackled. 'Ha, sweet! How many points do you get for that?'

When home-time came, the three Spy Toys

stood waiting in the playground for Auntie Roz to pick them up.

Flax felt a tug on his sleeve, and he turned to find Jack Dimpling standing shyly beside him.

'Hi.'

'Er, hi, Flax,' said Jack nervously. 'Me and the guys were wondering if you might want to come to our after-school club? It's pretty awesome. We do all kinds of cool sciency stuff.'

'Thanks,' said Flax. 'But I have to be getting home. Fish fingers tonight - I'm very excited.' Flax had researched the eating habits of children before the mission and decided that this was a good answer to give to such a question.

Jack persisted. 'I think you'd like it, Flax.

Repairing toys is just the tip of the iceberg.' He winked and handed Flax something.

Flax looked at the object. It was a bar of Chimpwick's Chocolate.

A horn hooted.

'Hey, nerdbrains!' yelled back Arabella as she and Dan ran towards Auntie Roz's car. 'Quit rabbiting! Our ride's here!'

Flax saw Jack wince at Arabella's unkind description of them. 'Sorry about her,' he muttered. Then he turned to Dan and Arabella. 'You guys go on,' he called. 'I'm going to hang out with my friend for a bit.'

CHAPTER FOUR

THE SECRET SOCIETY

Flax set off in the direction of the shed at the rear of the playground.

'Where are you going?' asked Jack.

'Science Club?'

Jack shook his head. 'That's for school time. The after-school club takes place somewhere *much* cooler. Come on.'

He led him to the bicycle shed. The other kids from Science Club were there on their bikes waiting for them.

'Looks like we have a new recruit,' Jack told the others. 'Flax'll ride with me.' He unchained a bicycle from a rack and sat at the front of its saddle, leaving room for Flax to squeeze in behind him. The children pedalled out of the school gates and along the street until they arrived at a wide expanse of waste ground enclosed by a wire fence. The fence had a gap in it and the children squeezed through, hunching over their bicycles.

Jack looked at Flax over his shoulder. 'The meeting place is about three miles away. Going through this bit of wasteland cuts a good chunk of time off the journey. Plus it means we can go as fast as we like.'

'And how fast is that?' asked Flax.

Jack laughed. 'I'm glad you asked.'

He flicked a switch on the handlebar of his bike. The other children did the same.

There was a roar of engines.

Flax felt the bike shudder – and then it and the other bikes suddenly surged forward at tremendous speed. He felt the hair on the head of his android bodysuit flutter and billow as the bikes zoomed across the waste ground at a dizzying rate, streaming fiery trails in their wake.

He whooped with delight. 'Rocket-powered bikes!' he yelled above the screaming engines. 'This is amazing! Astounding! Incredible!'

'Whoa there, Flax!' said Jack. 'Save a few of those cool adjectives for later. You'll need them.'

'Are these bikes made by Snaztacular Ultrafun?' asked Flax.

Jack snorted. 'Hardly! We did these modifications ourselves. These aren't kids' toys. This is *proper* tech!'

The group of rocket bikes crested a small hill and skidded to a halt at its summit. Jack pointed at a low, squarish building made of grey concrete at the bottom of the slope. Its boarded-up windows and empty, litter-strewn car park were not welcoming.

'What's that place?' asked Flax.

'The Learnatorium. Used to be an old science museum. It's where we hang out. Us and the others.'

'There's more of you?'

Jack grinned. 'A few. Let's go.'

The rocket bikes revved their engines, making a sound like a pride of angry lions, and thundered down the slope.

★ ★ ★

Arriving at the rear of the building, Jack and the others dismounted their bikes and entered through a fire escape. As they stepped into a darkened corridor, a pulsing blue light flashed over each of them. When it struck Flax, a screeching electronic alarm began to sound.

Flax's heart raced. 'What's that?'

'Don't worry,' said Jack. 'It's just a security scanner checking who we are. It doesn't recognise you so it's having a bit of a panic.' He tapped a few keys on a square metal box hanging from the wall. 'There. It knows you're a friend now. Follow me. You'll like this.'

He pushed open a door and he, Flax and the others stepped through into a large chamber, the main exhibition space of the museum. There were glass cases everywhere filled with interesting odds and ends – bits of meteorites, fossils, space-rocket engine parts, decades-old computers. Huge papier mâché representations of the planets hung from the ceiling.

'Wow,' muttered Flax softly. 'Awesome!'

At the far end of the chamber was a stage facing an audience of excited, chattering children. On the stage was a microphone on a stand and behind it a huge video screen. The air buzzed with anticipation. Jack and the others found some vacant seats and sat down.

'What's going on?' asked Flax.

'It's a special day today at **SIKBAG**,' said Jack. 'Our leader, April, has something big to announce.'

The eyebrows of Flax's android bodysuit formed themselves into a frown. 'Did you say sickbag?'

'**SIKBAG**,' explained Jack, stands for the Society of Intelligent Kids, Brain boxes And Geniuses. Sort of a secret society for brainy kids like us. I could tell straight away you were a potential member.'

'Members of **SIKBAG**!' boomed an amplified voice. 'Please show your appreciation for our leader, April Spume!'

The tiny figure of a girl with long pigtails strode out on to the stage and the crowd let out a cheer. She marched confidently up to the microphone and stood on her tiptoes to remove it from the stand. Behind, the screen showed a huge video image of her. She looked about seven years old.

'Who do grown-ups constantly push around?' she bellowed into the microphone. Her voice echoed off the building's concrete walls.

'Kids!' chorused back the audience.

'Who are the cleverest and best people in all the world?'

'Kids!'

'And who will one day rule the world?'

'Kids!'

Once again, the audience erupted into applause and cheers, stamping their feet so that the entire building shook. Flax found himself joining in with the audience responses. It was hard not to get swept up in the atmosphere of it all.

April Spume beamed at the audience.

'Welcome, all of you, to this very special meeting of **SIKBAG**. As you know, since the creation of our glorious organisation, we at **SIKBAG** have striven behind the scenes to make life better for our fellow kids. And look what we've achieved! Convincing the government to introduce a minimum level of pocket money for all children! Making it illegal to ruffle a kid's hair and say, "All right, sunshine?" without their written permission! Forcing all grandmothers to shave so kids don't get prickled when they give them a kiss!'

The crowd cheered each of these achievements in turn.

'Impressive though these victories are,' continued April, 'they are only the beginning.

For tonight, **SIKBAG** enters a bold new phase of operation! I have realised that there's one thing that always holds children back, one single thing that prevents them from achieving their true potential. One thing I intend to eliminate completely! Do you know what it is?'

'No!' chorused the crowd. 'Tell us!'

April raised a hand to the skies like a preacher. Behind her, the massive video image of her did the same. 'Fun!' she cried. 'I intend to eliminate all fun!'

There was a long silence.

Flax peered around the room. Children were staring at April, frowning and shrugging in puzzlement. *What* had she said?

'You want to get rid of all *fun*?' asked a

tiny voice from the back of the room.

'That's right!' said April. 'Clever kids like us could be ruling this entire planet right now if we weren't constantly distracted by doing fun things. Eating tooth-rotting sweets! Playing with silly toys! Watching stupid television programmes! Drinking unhealthy fizzy drinks! What a waste of time these activities are! That's why **SIKBAG** will now be stamping them all out! Completely!'

A gasp erupted from the crowd, followed by the soft hiss of shocked whispering.

April's eyes sparkled like shards of broken glass. She reached into the pocket of her dress and took out a tiny remote control device. The image of her on the giant video screen vanished and was replaced by that of a large and sturdy-looking building made of concrete and brick. 'This,' she said, 'is the factory of Snaztacular Ultrafun, the world's biggest manufacturer of toys. Toys! Those pointless, expensive, brain-numbing wastes of time that distract kids from what they should be doing – ruling the world! Well, watch this, my fellow **SIKBAG** members!' She jabbed a tiny button on her remote control. An eerie blue glow appeared around the factory and then, with a sudden

FLLIPPPPHHHHH!

noise, the entire building vanished, leaving nothing but a gaping hole in the ground.

The crowd gasped again.

April giggled. 'Behold! Our cleverest members have invented a *teleport device*! A machine that can take a thing apart into its smallest bits, beam them anywhere in the world, and then reassemble them perfectly in the new location. Our test on Chimpwick's Chocolate factory was a complete success and now we have stolen the Snaztacular Ultrafun factory too, teleporting it to the middle of the Sahara Desert where no one will ever find it!'

More gasps from the crowd. Most of them amazed, many of them scared.

Flax's heart began to beat very fast. 'Is she always like this?' he whispered to Jack.

The boy shook his head. 'Err – no. I think she's gone a tiny bit potty, actually.'

'But this is just the beginning!' April continued, a cold glint in her eye. 'Further targets are planned!'

Images of two more buildings appeared on the screen.

'The studios of Kidzland TV,' explained April. 'The channel that numbs kids' brains with its tedious, dumbed-down programmes like *Puppy Pirates* and *Kitten Kops*. And the bottling plant of Bogey Cola, the disgusting soft drink that kids seem addicted to these days. Soon, when world terror and panic have reached their maximum following the loss of Chimpwick's Chocolate and Snaztacular Ultrafun, we shall teleport away these other two places and the world's children will have lost four of their main sources of fun. Then eventually, no longer distracted, and under the command of us here at **SIKBAG**, kids will rise up and overthrow the grown-ups!'

She raised a fist in triumph, as if expecting to receive thunderous applause, but the only response was more shocked gasps and whispers.

'Is that really wise?' asked a tiny voice.

April frowned at the audience. 'What? Who said that?'

'Me.' It was a very small boy with angelic wisps of blond hair. He was sitting in the front row of the audience. 'Playing with toys is actually really good for children's intelligence. TV can be very educational, too. And surely there's nothing wrong with a bit of chocolate or fizzy pop every now and again? As a special treat?'

A few cautious murmurs of agreement came from the crowd.

April Spume smiled a sickly smile. 'I see,' she said very quietly.

A horrible hush descended on the room. It was like the split second of silence between a piano falling out of an upper-storey window and it hitting the pavement.

'What's your name?' she asked the boy in a friendly voice.

'Max,' said the boy. 'Max Pinker.'

'You like playing, Max. Would you like to play a game now?' asked April.

The boy nodded uncertainly. 'Erm, OK.'

April raised the microphone to her lips and said in a low voice, 'Sebastian? Young Max here would like to play thumb war.'

A squat boy with a thick mop of brown hair and a single black glove shuffled on to the stage.

'SIKBAG members,' said April, 'may I introduce my new bodyguard, Sebastian?'

Jack's eyes widened. 'I've seen that kid on the news,' he hissed at Flax. 'He's a dangerous criminal. Wanted on a hundred different counts of vandalism. They call him Sebastian Plum and his Stainless-Steel

Thumb!'

'And his *what*?' asked Flax.

'Just watch.'

'One, two, three, four, I declare a thumb war,' chanted Sebastian Plum gravely. He removed his black glove. The thumb of his right hand was a bright, glinting silver colour. He clambered off the stage, linked hands with Max, and the two began thumb wrestling. Max giggled with pleasure but then Sebastian pressed his shining metal thumb down hard on Max's hand. The little boy let out a long howl of pain.

'Let this be a lesson to you all!' thundered April into the microphone, jabbing a finger at the helpless form of Max as he writhed in agony under the pressure of Sebastian's steel thumb. 'I will not allow these traitorous outbursts! Release him, Sebastian.'

Sebastian Plum loosened his grip on Max's hand. The little blond boy moaned and sucked his sore knuckle.

'Anyone else care to chip in?' asked April, staring around the audience. Silence was the response. 'Good! And don't think of trying to leave. All exits and windows are sealed. Soon, you will be transported to our secret base, from where we **SIKBAG** members will form the ruling elite of the new kid-dominated world. We can't allow ourselves to be influenced by interfering adults, can we? None of you will ever see your parents again.'

The gasps that now came from the audience were very quiet and very, very frightened.

'And now,' said April brightly, 'time for nibbles.' She clicked her fingers and a spotlight lit up several long tables covered with plates of food. 'We have rice cakes, cucumber slices and muesli bars. Help yourselves, guys!'

The crowd of children rose to their feet, dazed and numb, and began to trudge slowly towards the tables of food.

'This plan of April's is absolutely horrible,' muttered Jack. 'We have to stop her. But how?'

'Help is at hand,' said Flax, and lifted the edge of the cloth covering one of the buffet tables. He swiftly dived underneath, motioning for Jack to follow.

'What are you doing under here?' asked Jack, crouching awkwardly in the confined space.

'Contacting some friends,' said Flax. He opened his school bag, took out a mobile phone and speedily began to compose a text.

TO: AUNTIE ROZ.

CHOC FACTORY TELEPORTED 2 SAHARA BY BRAINY KID GANG SIKBAG. SNAZ U'FUN FACTORY TOO! KIDZLAND TV, BOGEY COLA NEXT. THEIR HQ IS OLD LEARNATORIUM SCI MUSEUM.

'You see, I'm part of a secret organisation

myself,' he explained to Jack. 'One that will be very interested to hear what's happened here today.'

He thumbed the **SEND** key and let out a deep breath.

The tablecloth lifted and a face appeared, a brutish snout of a face.

'What are you doing under here?' rumbled Sebastian Plum.

Flax straightened up in surprise, banging his head on the underside of the table. There was a flash of blue light and a crackle of electricity.

Sebastian Plum rubbed his eyes. Where the boy with the mobile phone had hunched under the table there was now a very surprised-looking rabbit. Jack stared at him in disbelief.

Flax lifted his shades and gave Sebastian a friendly wink. 'Nearly Easter. Just hiding a few eggs.'

Sebastian reached out his black-gloved hand and grabbed Flax's wrist. 'You're in big trouble, big ears,' he rumbled.

CHAPTER FIVE

A FORTUNATE SHEET OF A4

DUKKA-DUKKA-DUKKA-DUKKA-DUKKA!

went the blades of the helicopter. Inside its cramped cockpit sat Dan and Arabella, now back to their usual selves after ditching their android bodysuits.

'Here!' called Arabella, waving a hand at the pilot. In the other hand she held a mobile phone open to its map application. 'We should be directly over the Learnatorium now!'

The helicopter slowed, wobbling, and began to hover.

Dan stared down at the ground and rubbed his hairy chin thoughtfully. 'Doesn't look much like a science museum. More like an enormous black hole. Unless it's *meant* to look like a black hole – you know, the ones in space. For educational purposes.'

Arabella groaned. 'It's gone, you furry fool! The whole science museum has been teleported away! Just like the Chimpwick's Chocolate and Snaztacular Ultrafun factories! **SIKBAG** must have realised we're on to them!'

'That means they've got Flax,' said Dan.

He and Arabella shared an anxious look. This was interrupted when Arabella's phone chirruped loudly. The rag doll answered it. Dan could hear Auntie Roz's booming voice above the noise of the helicopter blades.

'Chaps! Return to base immediately! We've just received a message from **SIKBAG**.'

★ ★ ★

Auntie Roz's tablet flickered into life. It showed a small girl with pigtails and eyes like two hard chips of ice. Standing behind her was a squat, tough-looking boy wearing a single black glove. Both stood in front of a window through which light streamed dramatically.

'Now, listen here, you grown-up idiots!' said the girl. 'My name is April Spume and I'm the leader of **SIKBAG**, the Society of Intelligent Kids, Brainboxes And Geniuses. We clever kids are fed up with

102

the way adults run the world. And we're fed up with the way you treat us children – distracting us with trivial things like chocolate and toys when we could be ruling the planet! So the fight back starts here. You may have noticed a certain couple of factories have gone walkabout. Well, that's just the beginning! With our teleporter we shall remove every obstacle that prevents children from realising their true potential – and then the world shall be ours!' The girl gave an evil chuckle. Behind her, the squat boy grinned repulsively.

The camera panned sharply to reveal Flax the rabbit bound tightly to a chair by thick ropes, a gag tied across his mouth. An indistinct furry shape was lumbering across the floor towards him.

'As you can see,' continued April, 'we've found a spy in our midst. Oh, little tip, guys: if you're going to go to the trouble of manufacturing an amazing android bodysuit disguise, don't have a label inside it saying **PROPERTY OF THE DEPARTMENT OF SECRET AFFAIRS**. Gives the game away a bit!'

Auntie Roz clapped a hand to her forehead. 'I must have words with Dr Willows,' she groaned.

'Send as many spies as you like,' taunted April. 'You'll never find us now that we've teleported our headquarters to a new location. Oh, and by the way, that creature you can see heading for the rabbit is my toy sloth, Victor. A toy who has been modified to eat *anything*. Plastic, rubber, glass – you name it. He's particularly fond of metal, however, and likes nothing better than chewing old robots to pieces.' The camera spun back to April and she jabbed a finger at its lens. 'So stay away! Or Victor's next meal will be robot rabbit pie! Understand?'

The screen went blank.

'What a charming little princess *she* is,' said Dan.

Arabella growled. 'That punk! I'd like to tie her pigtails to a runaway train. Who the heck is she, anyway?'

Auntie Roz consulted a tablet device. 'The girl is April Elizabeth Spume. Seven years old. Daughter of a pair of rocket scientists. A pupil at St Jim's Boarding School for Gifted and Annoying Children but seems to spend most of her time skiving off and taking part in fiendish plots. Rumour has it she was one of the gang of kids who tried to kidnap the popular children's TV character Callum the Halibut last year, but it was never proved. Quite the little handful. The boy standing behind her is Sebastian Rodriguez Plum. It seems he lost one thumb at a safari park, trying to feed cheese-and-onion crisps to a leopard, and had it replaced with a stainless-steel version – the thumb, I mean, not the leopard. He can do an awful lot of damage with that metal thumb, and he's used it to vandalise everything from aeroplanes to zoos. Sebastian's immensely strong, not very bright and just as mean as April.'

'The no-good, snot-nosed, jumped-up little monsters,' hissed Arabella savagely.

'That's what you say about *all* children,' muttered Dan.

'How are we going to stop them?' asked Arabella. 'That nerd-palace science museum they hang out in could have been teleported anywhere on the planet.'

'It's impossible to say where they are,' said Auntie Roz grimly. 'Dr Willows analysed every aspect of that video message – digital stamp, file format, colour spectrum, everything – and hasn't found the slightest clue to indicate where it was filmed. It was emailed to us from an untraceable web server, too. We're completely stumped.'

Dan frowned. 'You mean you don't know exactly which street in Paris it was filmed in?'

Auntie Roz blinked. 'How do you know it was filmed in Paris? Is it something to do with the type of video camera they used? Is it the precise angle of the sunlight at the time it was filmed? Or the background sounds?'

Dan shook his head. 'Not really. It's more to do with the fact you can see the Eiffel Tower through the window.'

'*What???*'

Dan took Auntie Roz's tablet device and scrolled back through the video until the view through the window behind April and Sebastian was at its clearest. 'There,' he said, pointing a paw at a familiar-looking black spire visible above some rooftops. 'I'm no expert on geography but I do believe this structure here, jutting up over the other buildings, is the Eiffel Tower. And that's in Paris, isn't it? Like I say, I'm no expert. In fact, I'm pretty sure I only learned it at school this morning.'

Auntie Roz whooped with delight. She would have picked Dan up and kissed him, had she not thought this would dent her image as a strict, no-nonsense boss. She looked around for some underling she could order to pick Dan up and kiss him, but to her annoyance there were none around. 'Top work, Dan!' she declared, beaming. 'I'm amazed Dr Willows missed that. She's quite the genius herself. Although I'm starting to wonder if she's quite as intelligent as I first thought ...'

'She'd probably notice a lot more if she spent less time playing on her phone,' Arabella said, with a smirk.

'We need to get to France really fast to stop this bunch of brainy brats,' said Dan.

'And we need to be pretty sneaky about how we do it, too,' chipped in Arabella. 'Or our brainy bunny ends up as a swift snack for a super-savage sloth.'

'Can you get us on the next flight to Paris?' asked Dan.

'I can do better than that,' said Auntie Roz. 'Follow me.'

★ ★ ★

She led them to the car park at the rear of the **DEPARTMENT OF SECRET AFFAIRS** building. It was a cold, clear evening and a weary sun was smearing orange light across the horizon. Dr Willows was waiting for them. Once again her attention was fixed on the screen of her phone, thumbs paddling away madly.

Auntie Roz coughed meaningfully.

Dr Willows looked up in surprise and then hurriedly put her phone away. 'Oh, you're here. Great.'

'What are we doing out here?' asked Arabella.

'Time is short,' said Auntie Roz. 'We need to get you to Paris immediately. Our fastest helicopter would take a couple of hours. But Dr Willows has created something that can get you there much faster. Dr Willows? This is your chance to redeem yourself after your recent blunder.'

Dr Willows flushed deep red. 'Oh, yes. Totally. Sorry, guys.' She opened a briefcase and took out a blank sheet of A4 paper. She handed it to Dan. 'Take this,' she said. 'And look after it. It's the only one of its kind in existence. I hope it serves you well.'

Dan and Arabella exchanged a look. You didn't need to be a mind reader to know they were thinking words like 'twerp' and 'nitwit'.

'I'm pretty sure,' said Dan, eyeing the sheet of paper, 'that you can get these at most high-street stationers.'

'Not like this,' said Dr Willows with an intriguing grin. She took what looked like an ordinary pencil from the briefcase and passed it to Arabella. 'Dan, put the paper on the ground. Arabella, write something

on the paper with the pencil. Anything –
it doesn't matter what. It's all about the
reaction between the two substances.'

With a sigh, Dan placed the sheet of paper
on the ground. Arabella knelt and wrote
**DR WiLLOWS HAS THE WIT AND
iNTELLiGENCE OF A DISCARDED
CRiSP PACKET** on it in bold letters.

'Now what?'

'Stand back,' said Dr Willows, 'and watch!'

Dan and Arabella stepped back, folding
their arms and shaking their heads.

There was a sudden rumbling noise. The
sheet of A4 paper began to bulge and burp
and burst, and then with startling speed it
split itself in half like the layers of a tissue
being pulled apart. These two layers then

divided into four layers, then eight, then sixteen. Within a few moments there were hundreds of sheets of paper covering nearly the whole car park. At some crucial point the sheets of paper all bulged and burped and burst as one and folded themselves neatly together into a sleek, dart-like object that was slightly bigger than a family car. It glowed pinkly in the warm light of sunset.

Dan and Arabella's eyes popped in astonishment.

'It's a paper plane!' they cried in unison.

Dr Willows nodded. 'A super-smart, cellulose-fibre, hexi-silicon paper plane, to be precise. Hop in. You'll find the controls a doddle to use.'

'I call pilot's seat!' cried Arabella, and

raced to clamber into the paper plane's cockpit. Dan followed and slid into the seat next to her. As he did so he noticed the words Arabella had written – **DR WiLLOWS HAS THE WIT AND iNTELLiGENCE OF A DISCARDED CRiSP PACKET** – etched on one wing of the plane.

'Don't forget this,' called Dr Willows, and tossed the pencil into the cockpit. Arabella caught it. 'At the other end is an eraser. Rub out the words you wrote and the plane will unfold into a single sheet again. Good luck, guys.'

Arabella swiped a touchscreen on the cockpit instrument panel. The plane's engines began to whine.

'Just enter the required destination into

the navigation computer,' said Dr Willows.

'Got it!' called Arabella, and speedily typed the word '**PARIS**'. 'Then what?'

'You see that big button marked **FLY**?'

'Yep?'

'Well, what are you waiting for?'

CHAPTER SIX

PLANE STUPID

'Hold still!' cried April Spume at the crowd of unhappy children assembled before her in the Learnatorium's main hall. 'How can I program the exact details of the next cargo to be teleported when people keep shuffling about and fidgeting? Honestly, you're like a troop of naughty chimps.' She twisted a dial on the teleport machine, which looked a little like a large metal dish, and gave a satisfied grunt. 'Right. Good. Listen up, everyone. You will shortly be transported directly to the new **SIKBAG** secret base, from which we shall begin our reign of terror over the adult world. You will find the new base elegantly designed, fully equipped and filled with countless stimulating activities for young minds, making it the perfect venue from which to rule the planet. Oh, and I hope you've all brought jumpers and scarves because it's in Antarctica. Bit nippy there, I know, but it's a heck of a good hiding place. See you later, guys!'

Before anyone could respond, April twisted the dial and the crowd of children vanished in a flash of blue light.

April gave a satisfied nod. All she had to do now before she joined the other **SIKBAG** members was sort out a couple of *tiny* problems …

★ ★ ★

Like a shining white arrow, the paper plane streaked through the hazy air above London.

Dan stared down in wonderment. 'Wow! I've never travelled this fast in my life!'

But when he turned to Arabella, he found her scrolling through a list of commands on the touchscreen, engrossed in some task.

'What are you doing?'

'This ain't that fast,' she snorted. 'I don't

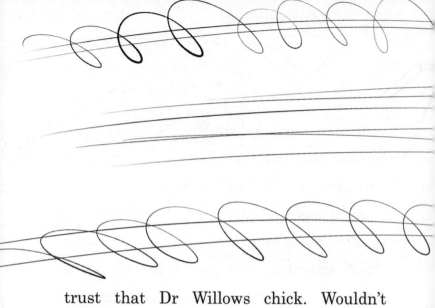

trust that Dr Willows chick. Wouldn't surprise me if she's put some kind of safety limiter on this plane's speed and manoeuvrability. If I can find the manual override for the automatic pilot and take control myself, I bet I can get us to Paris in half the time.'

'But if there's a safety limiter, it's there to keep us safe,' reasoned Dan. 'Which means turning it off could be very

DANGEROOOOOOOOOOOUS!'

The plane suddenly lurched violently and shot forward with a massive burst of speed.

'Ha ha!' chortled Arabella, clutching a joystick control, which had just slid out of a small hatch in the cockpit display panel. 'Found it!'

'I hope you know what you're doing,' whined Dan as the world blurred around them.

"Course I do, furbag. We're flying nearly twice as fast we were!'

Dan pointed through the cockpit windscreen. 'Er, yeah. But I can't help noticing that we're also now flying directly towards the *sea*.'

Arabella frowned and checked the view through the windscreen.

The sparkling blue waters of the English Channel were approaching at high speed.

'Oh, that's the sea,' said Arabella with a guilty laugh. 'I thought it was the sky. They're both blue, you see, so no wonder I got a little –'

'Pull up now!' screamed Dan. 'Quickly!'

Arabella yanked hard on the joystick. 'Controls aren't responding. We're going too fast. Gimme a minute here ...'

'Turn the automatic pilot back on,' yelled

Dan. 'Now! I don't want to swim to Paris!'

'It's OK,' said Arabella, the choppy, churning surface of the sea thundering towards them at terrifying speed. 'I'm pretty sure I can do this ...'

Dan reached over and swiped a paw across the cockpit touchscreen.

Immediately the plane pulled out of its nosedive and the joystick control retracted back into the display panel. The paper aircraft continued peacefully on its way. Dan let out a long, relieved sigh.

Arabella shrugged. 'Fine. We'll do it the boring way.'

Not long later, the paper plane touched down on a wide, tree-lined avenue in the centre of Paris, much to the surprise of the many tourists ambling along it. The two toys hopped out. Dan took the pencil Dr Willows had given them and carefully erased the words Arabella had written on the wing. There was a swish, a whir and a flap and the plane rapidly unfolded itself into what looked like a sheet of ordinary A4 paper. Arabella folded it up and stuffed it the pocket of her dress for safekeeping.

She and Dan dashed off along the avenue. Looming ahead of them was the Eiffel Tower, whose massive tapering form surveyed the busy Parisian streets like a friendly giant. Dan waved a paw at a huge, elegant-looking building. 'There,' he said. 'That's where they must have filmed the video. The top floor of that building is the only place in Paris that gives the correct view of the Eiffel Tower.'

'You think those **SIKBAG** creeps teleported the entire Learnatorium inside that place?'

Dan gave a shrug. 'There's no other explanation.'

They pushed open the tall glass door of the building and rushed inside. It turned out to be a vast shoe shop, with footwear of every imaginable sort displayed on beautiful metal stands and lit dramatically with spotlights.

The toys raced to a door at the back of the shop. They opened it, ran up a flight of stairs, pushed open another door and finally emerged on to the roof of the building. It was flat, made of greyish concrete, dotted with dirty puddles of rainwater – and completely empty.

'I don't understand,' said Dan. 'This is the place. It has to be. Where are they?'

Arabella shrugged. 'Looks like we're too late. They must have teleported away.'

Dan shook his head. 'Something's not right. We're at the correct angle to see the Eiffel Tower, but the tower itself looks different, much thinner and darker in colour. Almost as if ...' He gasped and snapped his fingers. 'Of course!'

'What?' asked Arabella.

'They were never here!' cried Dan. 'They weren't in Paris at all! That April Spume's as sneaky as a sockful of snakes!'

'How can that be true?' said Arabella. 'Where else do they have an Eiffel Tower?'

'I know where!' said Dan.

CHAPTER SEVEN

WHEN THE SUN GOES DOWN

Flax's eyes snapped open. He found himself wedged in a tight space with pink, sloping walls lined with sticky slime.

'Yuck,' he muttered. He tried to move but his limbs were stuck fast in the gloopy substance. 'Jack? Jack? Are you there?'

'I'm right here, Flax,' replied Jack. His voice was muffled and seemed to come from the other side of one of the sloping pink walls. 'In the other nostril.'

'In the other *what*?'

'After she used you in the video message, April asked Sebastian to stick us both somewhere to keep us out of mischief. So he bunged us inside the interactive model of the human nose in the Learnatorium biology exhibit. You must have hit your head and passed out.'

'You mean we're trapped inside a giant model of a human nose?'

'Yes,' said Jack. 'Trapped, not to put too fine a point on it, in artificial snot.'

Flax grimaced. 'I'll never get this stuff out

of my fur.'

'Ah, yes,' said Jack. 'I couldn't help but notice that you're, well, a *rabbit*. Not a schoolboy.'

'I'm a spy,' said Flax. 'Investigating the missing chocolate factory.'

'This plan of April's is absolutely abominable!' said Jack. 'We have to stop her somehow.'

'Of course,' said Flax. 'But in a funny way you have to sort of admire her, too. Fun *does* get in the way of you doing important things. If my two colleagues spent less time enjoying themselves and more time concentrating on their work, we'd catch a lot more bad guys.'

'But fun's important, too!' said Jack. 'You can't work all the time. Life would be unbearable without a game or a laugh or a bit of chocolate every now and then. I saw your face when you got off that rocket bike. Grinning from ear to ear, you were! Don't tell me that wasn't worth doing.'

'I have to admit,' said Flax, 'that was pretty cool.'

'Exactly! And you also seemed to be having a good time playing **TURBO BADGER** this afternoon, if I remember right!'

Flax gave a nervous cough. 'That wasn't playing. I was sharpening up my hand-eye coordination.'

Jack snorted. '*Of course you were.* So tell me, Mr Spy Rabbit, how the heck are we going to escape from this nose?'

Flax closed his eyes and tried to think. 'This is a multi-million-pound interactive exhibit designed to exactly model the functions of a human nose, right?'

'Right.'

'And how do noses expel small foreign objects that have got lodged inside them?'

Jack laughed delightedly. 'With a sneeze! But how? We're stuck fast.'

'My arms and legs may be stuck,' said Flax. 'But my ears aren't!'

He reached out with one of his long, white ears and gently tickled the slimy surface of the nearest pink wall. At once, there was a sound of rushing air and the interior of the huge nose began to shake ...

'I think it's working!' cried Jack.

'Brace yourself,' said Flax. 'I think this is going to be a big one ...'

AACCCHHHoooOOO!

With the force of a hurricane, Jack and Flax shot out of the nostrils of the enormous nose and flew like bullets across the central exhibition gallery of the Learnatorium.

Flax bounced off the side of an antique steam engine and skittered to the floor.

'Oh my flipping ears and whiskers,' he muttered to himself, and clambered to his feet. He peered around. 'Jack? Jack?'

There was no reply. And then from gloomy silence rose the distant grumbling roar of the mechanical sloth, Victor ...

★ ★ ★

The paper plane zoomed over the green fields of England, making a V-formation of passing geese swerve and honk in annoyance.

Dan gave Arabella a nudge. 'Right there. See?' he said, raising his voice to be heard above the throb of the plane's engines.

Arabella looked down and saw a cluster

of tiny buildings. 'Weird!' she exclaimed. 'We must be higher than I thought.'

The teddy bear shook his head. 'Look again! It's the **WORLDLAND MODEL VILLAGE**! Miniature models of the world's capital cities! The kids at the primary school were going on a trip there, remember? Look, there's a scale model of the Eiffel Tower!'

Dan pointed to a small clump of trees not far from the entrance gate to the model village. 'Put us down there.'

The gate was locked firmly with a chunky metal padlock. A neatly printed sign taped to it declared:

WE ARE VERY SORRY BUT

WORLDLAND MODEL VILLAGE IS TEMPORARILY CLOSED. WE HOPE THAT DOESN'T SPOIL YOUR DAY!

'That proves the place has been taken over by children,' said Dan. 'Adults would never go to the trouble of making a sign that looks that neat. And they'd probably have spelt "your" wrongly too.' He crushed the padlock in his fist as easily as a marshmallow and pushed open the gate.

'That way,' said Arabella, pointing at a model Eiffel Tower poking above some distant rooftops.

They dashed through a scale model of New York City, trampled over most of Madrid and finally arrived at the outskirts of Paris. The Learnatorium science museum was parked somewhat disrespectfully over a large part of the model city (and a good portion of Dublin, too), squashing the tiny buildings flat.

'OK, mission recap,' said Arabella as they reached the door. 'Objective one: rescue Flax. Objective two: take down **SIKBAG**. You with me, fuzzball?'

Dan nodded. 'Roger that.' He reached for the door handle.

Arabella seized his arm. 'Careful, nitwit! Those brainy brats might be expecting company.'

'You mean they might have laid traps?' asked Dan, suddenly wary.

Arabella nodded.

'I'll be careful,' said Dan. He forced open the locked door as quietly as he could and stepped inside. Immediately, a Formula One racing car fell from the ceiling on top of him, bounced harmlessly off his super-strong head and clattered across the floor of the museum's entrance lobby.

Dan turned to Arabella. 'Seems you were right.'

Arabella snorted. 'Why do you think I'm letting you go first?'

The museum appeared to be deserted. The only sound was the quiet echo of the toys' footsteps as they padded across the entrance lobby to study a map of the museum.

Arabella tapped a finger on a second-floor area of the map that said **STAFF ONLY** in official letters. 'In the video, it looked like they were in an office. I reckon this is where they're hiding out.'

Dan nodded. 'Let's take the stairs. No doubt the lift will be booby-trapped, too.'

They raced to a wide marble staircase at the back of the entrance lobby. As soon as they set foot on the first step, there was a deep booming noise, and a torrent of brightly coloured balls of different sizes began to cascade down the stairs towards them.

There was something oddly familiar about the markings on each ball: crater-like circular patches and great bands of colour that looked like swirling clouds.

'They're model planets!' said Arabella, ducking as a miniature Mars bounced over her head. 'How typical of nerds to try and kill us in a way that's also educational!'

Dan jumped to avoid a large orange-striped ball resembling the planet Jupiter that was thundering down the stairs towards him. 'Watch out for that model Saturn!' he called to Arabella. 'Its rings look sharp!'

Arabella sidestepped Saturn and hopped to avoid a swarm of small asteroids that were rattling noisily down the steps like dried peas.

And then, as suddenly as it had begun, the rain of planets ceased. Dan and Arabella paused to catch their breath. They were halfway up the staircase. They quickly resumed their climb but after a moment Arabella suddenly stopped with a gasp.

'Dan! Wait!'

'What?'

'A horrible thought has just occurred.'

'Do share it,' said Dan with a sigh. 'I can never hear enough horrible thoughts.'

Arabella counted on her fingers. 'Neptune, Uranus, Saturn, Jupiter, the asteroids, Mars, Earth, Venus and Mercury. We've had models of all the major bodies in the solar system except one.'

Dan blinked. 'Do you mean Pluto?'

Arabella shook her head. 'That's not even a planet! Think bigger. An awful lot bigger.'

'You mean ... ?'

Arabella nodded – and at that very moment there appeared at the top of the staircase a truly enormous yellow ball.

'The sun!'

Slowly, then with gathering speed, the model sun hurtled down the staircase towards them.

'It's coming too fast!' cried Arabella. 'We can't outrun it! I suddenly feel sorry for all the bowling pins I've knocked down over the years.'

'Flatten yourself against the wall,' called Dan. 'It's our only chance.'

The two toys flattened themselves against the walls and the enormous model of the sun tore between them at tremendous speed, missing them both by the merest smidgen. They watched, scarcely able to believe their good fortune, as the giant yellow sphere bounced to the bottom of the staircase and –

CRRRRRANNNNXXX SSCCCCHHHHHHHHH!

– smashed itself into the side of the ticket desk.

Dan raised his eyebrows. 'Not the most relaxing of sunsets.'

'Come on, furball,' said Arabella. 'Job to do.'

They raced to the top of the stairs and

found themselves at the start of a long corridor lined with stuffed animals in cases. At the end stood an open door with a sign on it reading: **PRIVATE. STAFF ONLY.**

'Like a door's gonna stop the strongest teddy in the world getting in,' sniggered Arabella. She leaned against a case containing a stuffed rabbit, but to her surprise the stuffed rabbit inside jumped in alarm. 'Flax!' cried Arabella. 'What are you doing in there?'

'Hiding,' said the robot rabbit, lifting off the cover of the case and leaping to the floor to join his colleagues. 'I've been trying to find my friend, Jack, but he seems to have vanished. How did you chaps get here?'

'Long story short,' said Arabella, 'we found you, rescued you and now we have to kick the bad guys' butts.'

'Oh good,' said Flax. 'That's my favourite bit.'

A squat, dark figure suddenly stepped out of the shadows and stood before them.

'Speaking of which …' muttered Arabella.

CHAPTER EIGHT

A BIT OF A PICKLE

Sebastian Plum removed the black glove from his right hand. His stainless-steel thumb glimmered in the gloomy corridor.

'One, two, three four,' he droned gravely, 'I declare a thumb war!'

He marched towards them, hand outstretched, thumb bobbing up and down hungrily.

'I'll deal with this little squirt,' said Dan. He strode purposefully towards Sebastian and locked hands with him.

'Watch out!' cried Flax. 'He's stronger than he looks!'

'So am I!' said Dan with a smile. 'This shouldn't take a minu–

ΑΑΑΑΑΑΑ**ΑGGHHHH!'**

A terrible pain seared into his paw where Sebastian Plum was pressing down on it with his stainless-steel thumb.

'Ha ha!' laughed Sebastian in his deep voice. 'You may be strong, little teddy bear, but nothing is as strong as my stainless-steel thumb!'

He pressed down hard on Dan's paw. Dan let out a cry of agony and sank to his knees.

'True,' gasped Dan. 'Your thumb is extremely strong, even compared with mine. But there's something about me you don't know yet.'

'Is there?' snorted Sebastian. 'What?'

'The rest of me is strong, too.'

Dan suddenly sprang to his feet and grasped Sebastian by his collar. Caught off guard, the boy released his grip on Dan's paw. Dan spun the boy around a few times and then slid him at tremendous speed across the shiny wooden floor of the corridor, where he smashed into a case containing a family of stuffed field mice, who tumbled down on to his head. He groaned quietly.

The three Spy Toys now stood before the door marked **PRIVATE. STAFF ONLY**.

Dan looked at his colleagues. 'We ready, guys?'

Arabella cracked her knuckles. 'Ready as an extra-large helping of Ready Pie with generous lashings of thick, creamy Ready Sauce,' she said, adding, 'That means yes,' when she saw Dan and Flax's confused expressions.

Dan kicked open the door and they entered the room.

There they found April Spume sitting in a huge armchair behind a desk. On her lap was the slumbering form of her pet sloth, Victor. Otherwise, she was alone. She gave the three toys a charming smile.

'I was going to say, "I've been expecting you",' she said, 'but you've taken so flipping long to get here that I practically gave up all hope. You are some kind of secret-agent types sent here to stop me, I suppose?'

'That's right, sweetheart,' growled Arabella.

April snorted. 'You lot really are the most pathetic bunch of amateur-ish losers I've ever had the misfortune to encounter!'

The three Spy Toys exchanged a look of irritation.

'People who say things like that about us,' said Dan quietly, 'usually end up very sorry indeed.'

'Oh, button it,' said April, and flicked a switch on her desk.

There was a hum of electricity and suddenly Dan, Flax and Arabella found themselves flying across the room and slamming painfully into a large horseshoe-shaped hunk of metal.

'Just a simple, immensely powerful electromagnet,' explained April. 'All you need to keep three stupid robotic toys out of mischief. Doesn't exactly take a genius to work that out. And now he's been enhanced with his new plastic skeleton, dear Victor here is not affected by it.' She stroked the sloth's head soothingly, then lifted him off her lap and placed him on the floor. She pointed at the three helpless toys pinned to the electromagnet. 'Dinner time! I've found you three lovely fresh robots to chew on!'

The sloth turned his two small eyes towards Flax and the others and smiled a slow, slothful grin, revealing a mouthful of sharp and distinctly un-slothful teeth. He began to lumber towards them very, very slowly.

'What have you done with all the **SIKBAG** kids?' yelled Flax.

'They've been teleported to my secret pyramid in Antarctica, of course,' replied April with a smirk. 'It's the new **SIKBAG HQ** from which we'll rule the world. Nothing says evil organisation like a big secret pyramid in the Antarctic, I always think.' She swivelled around on her seat to face a complicated bank of electronic equipment. 'Now, just a couple of chores: using the teleporter to send the Kidzland TV studios and Bogey Cola bottling plant to the Sahara ...' She flicked a few switches and twisted several dials. 'There! And now to hop over to Antarctica myself!'

She hopped off her chair and on to a blue circle painted on the floor. 'Victor, dear, do join me in the new HQ when you've finished your meal. Just press the blue button. Toodles!'

An eerie blue glow appeared around April, and then with a sudden **FLIPPPHHH** noise, she vanished.

Victor the sloth continued to lumber towards the toys. He licked his lips.

'This is a bit of a pickle,' said Flax. 'I have an EMP emitter in my pocket that could knock out this sloth, but unfortunately I can't reach it because my arms are stuck to this magnet. Anyone else got any plans?'

'I'd like to learn how to play the piano one day,' said Arabella.

'I meant escape plans,' said Flax.

'Oh. Er, no. Not yet. You got anything, furball?'

Dan tried to shake his head but found even that was impossible with the electromagnet holding him. 'Nope – but I'll definitely let you know if I do think of anything.'

'Well, you'd better hurry up,' said Arabella. 'Because that sloth is gonna be nibbling our toes off in …'

'…about three hours, by the looks of things!' said Dan, and he and Arabella laughed.

Flax gave a sigh.

In the frozen wastes of Antarctica, deep within a vast, gleaming pyramid made of glass and steel, the members of **SIKBAG** watched as April Spume materialised with an eerie blue glow. Surveying their gloomy faces, she gave a scathing snort.

'Missing home, are we? Ha, don't worry. You'll soon cheer up once we become rulers of the entire world!'

The Spy Toys watched as Victor the sloth continued his weary trudge.

'Maybe he'll fall asleep before he gets to us,' mused Flax.

'Or die of old age,' said Dan.

'If *he* doesn't, *we* might,' said Arabella. 'I take it we're still drawing a blank in the bright ideas department?'

'Well, I've got nothing,' said Dan. 'Flax?'

'Still working on it,' said Flax.

'Oh, fabulous,' muttered Arabella. 'So we're still all going to die and these pint-size Einsteins are going to take over the world and turn it into one big mental arithmetic lesson.'

''Fraid so,' said Flax.

'I had no idea dying would be this dull,' said Dan. 'I always assumed we'd go doing something cool. Fighting alien monsters or something. Not being gnawed on by some moth-eaten sloth with a taste for scrap metal. In about two and half hours' time.' He let out a sigh at the unfairness of it all.

There was an unexpected click. The electromagnet stopped humming and the three Spy Toys suddenly dropped to the floor.

'Jack!' cried Flax as the small, wiry-haired boy emerged from behind the electromagnet brandishing a plug. 'Where did you come from?'

'After we got sneezed out, I got lost so I hid inside the steam-engine exhibit. After a bit, everything went quiet so I came looking for you.'

'Watch out, kid!' cried Arabella. 'That sloth is getting ready to take a bite out of your leg.'

'Ha, not a problem,' said Jack, and swiftly flicked the switch behind Victor's ear to **OFF**. The sloth slumped to the floor, motionless.

Flax raced to the teleport controls and began to examine them.

'Can you work this thing, cottontail?' asked Arabella.

Flax's nose twitched. 'I believe I can. If I do this' – he twisted a dial violently – 'it should bring back the last thing it teleported.'

Once again there was a **FLIPPPHHH** noise and April reappeared in the circle with a shimmer of blue light. She folded her arms and glared at the Spy Toys. 'What's the big idea trying to mess up my plan, you bunch of interfering clots!'

'April,' said Flax calmly, 'the game's up. Just surrender.'

The little girl cackled wildly. 'It's not over yet, you long-eared loser.' She rolled up her sleeve to reveal a thick metal wristband into which a red button was set. She jabbed it and something resembling a rucksack made of shiny metal began to assemble itself on her back. There was a whine of engines. 'I never go anywhere without my emergency jetpack! Laters, guys!' She grabbed the unconscious form of Victor the sloth from the floor and pressed the red button on the wristband again. With a mighty

WHOOOSSHH,

a stream of fire shot from the jetpack's engines and April and Victor smashed through the window and up into the sky.

Arabella groaned in frustration. 'The little brat's getting away.'

Flax was still staring at the teleport controls. He was not a happy rabbit. 'We have another problem, too. Rather a big one as it goes.'

'What now?' asked Dan.

'When I requested the teleport to bring back the last thing it had transported, I accidentally asked it bring back the last *two* things it had transported.'

'So what does that mean?'

'It means,' said Flax, 'that the entire Bogey Cola bottling plant is going to teleport into this room in a few seconds' time.'

'*Ouch*,' said Arabella. 'Sounds like a bit of a squeeze.'

'Now would be an excellent time to run for our lives,' suggested Flax.

CHAPTER NINE

LOOSE ENDS

Jack and the three Spy Toys raced out of the Learnatorium with seconds to spare before the building's walls exploded in showers of rubble. An entire fizzy drink bottling plant had appeared out of nowhere within the teleport room, bursting the Learnatorium apart like an overinflated balloon.

Jack noticed a familiar shape parked near the rear of the wrecked museum. 'My rocket bike!' he cried. 'It must have got teleported here with the Learnatorium!'

'Hop on it, kid,' commanded Arabella.

'And get the heck out of here. Contact the **DEPARTMENT OF SECRET AFFAIRS**. Tell them to send help. Who'd have thought one pigtailed pipsqueak could be so hard to beat?'

Flax squinted into the sky. April Spume was a tiny dot receding into the distance. 'How on earth are we going to catch her?'

'I know just how, big ears,' said Arabella, and removed the sheet of folded A4 from her pocket.

Flax snorted. 'What are you going to do with that? Make a paper plane?'

★ ★ ★

Like a streaking white comet, the paper plane whizzed and swished and soared over the **WORLDLAND MODEL VILLAGE** in pursuit of April Spume. They chased her over a tiny Oslo, across a miniature Abu Dhabi, past an itsy-bitsy Prague and around a pygmy Amsterdam. April's jetpack was swift and highly manoeuvrable, forcing the plane to make sharp twists and dives and swerves.

She hid behind a model of the Leaning Tower of Pisa and watched as the plane zoomed past.

'Fools!' she said with a chuckle, and sped away in the opposite direction. But then she heard the roar of the plane's jet engines and knew they were right behind her once again.

She searched around in vain for a hiding place, looked upwards, and suddenly smiled a small, self-satisfied smile.

On board the paper plane, Flax jabbed a finger at a large grey cloud floating peacefully overhead. 'She's going to try and lose us in there! Head for it as fast as you can!'

'You got it, bunny boy,' said Arabella, and pulled back on the throttle.

The paper plane sped upwards, gaining on the tiny, distant shape of April Spume, and slipped into the feathery greyness of the cloud.

Dan peered around. 'Any sign of her?'

Suddenly, an alarm hooted.

'Oh great,' muttered Arabella.

'What's up?'

'That little clever clogs,' growled Arabella. 'I bet she knew this would happen.'

'What's going on?' demanded Flax.

'What's the worst thing that can happen to a paper plane?' said Arabella. 'It can get wet!'

'*It can what?*'

Around them, the sleek surfaces of the plane were turning a mottled grey colour and starting to crumple …

★ ★ ★

Hovering in her jetpack on the other side of the cloud, April watched as the Spy Toys' paper plane began to plummet earthwards, its waterlogged wings fluttering uselessly.

She flicked the switch behind Victor's ear to **ON**. 'You'll like this! Look at those ridiculous toys falling to their doom!'

The mechanical sloth gave an amused grunt.

The soggy plane clipped the top of a large sign protruding from the roof of the Bogey Cola Plant. The sign read:

BOGEY COLA – THE SOFT DRINK EVERYONE PICKS!

This slight collision slowed the plane's descent and sent it spinning and tumbling to the ground in a soggy heap. The sign toppled forward on to the bottling plant's huge spherical storage tank and a massive torrent of fizzing green liquid began to gush out.

Dan, Arabella and Flax emerged groggily

from the soggy wreckage of the paper plane. 'I really must mention this little design flaw to Dr Willows next time I see her,' muttered Arabella.

Flax pointed, wide-eyed, at the fizzing tidal wave of green liquid heading straight for them. All he could think of to say was, 'Eep.' He, Dan and Arabella sprinted towards the model of the Eiffel Tower and shinned their way to the top, hoping to escape the rising tide of Bogey Cola.

High above, April Spume roared with laughter and hugged her mechanical sloth. 'Oh, what fun, Victor! Look at those tiny idiots run! The whole of **WORLDLAND MODEL VILLAGE** is filling with Bogey Cola!'

Flax watched April's jetpack zigzag overhead. 'What does that remind me of?' he murmured to himself.

'Is it our imminent death, by any chance?' snapped Arabella.

'It's a cabbage!' cried Flax delightedly. 'She looks just like a flying cabbage!'

Dan and Arabella exchanged one of their what-the-heck-is-the-daft-bunny-babbling-on-about-now? looks.

Flax reached into his school bag and drew out the EMP emitter. He pointed it upwards, tracking the course of April's jetpack.

'You'll never hit her with a burst from that thing,' snorted Arabella. 'She's moving way too fast.'

Flax winked at her. 'Did I ever tell you guys that I'm a natural at **TURBO BADGER**?'

Dan and Arabella exchanged a second look.

Flax activated the EMP emitter. There was a loud buzz, and high above them, the engines of April's jetpack suddenly spluttered and then fell silent. April began to lose height.

Flax, Arabella and Dan watched as April Spume and her mechanical sloth plummeted from the sky and plopped into the rising ocean of fizzing soft drink.

After a second, she bobbed to the surface like a cork. 'Help!' she called in a frantic gargle of a voice. 'I may be super-clever but I've never actually taken the time to learn to swim! Help me!' A sudden surging current of

Bogey Cola snatched her away and carried her towards the model of London, where it wedged her painfully between Big Ben and the House of Commons. Victor the sloth clambered on to April's head, fearful of the rising tide of frothing green liquid.

Dan stared down at the fizzing green waves. 'So what do you reckon? We swim for it?'

Before either of his colleagues could answer, there was a roar of rotor blades and a huge helicopter swung into view. Two hatches opened in its side, revealing the smiling faces of Jack, Auntie Roz and Dr Willows.

Auntie Roz raised her eyebrows. 'Need a lift?'

'So sorry about the plane malfunction, guys,' said Dr Willows, blushing hotly. 'I did make a note somewhere to include a layer of waterproofing but I think I must have got distracted and forgotten ...'

The three Spy Toys leaped aboard. Flax pointed towards the model Parliament where April was squirming between the famous landmarks. 'She's behind all this. We need to get her out.'

'How do we do that?' asked Dan.

'Hold on to one of my legs and one of Arabella's and dangle us out of the helicopter.'

'And then?'

'We each grab a pigtail.'

★ ★ ★

Safely back in their luxurious apartment in Mulbarton Street once again, the rabbit, the teddy bear and the rag doll waited impatiently by their huge video screen. No adventure was truly over, they knew, until Auntie Roz had had her say.

True to form, the screen flickered into life and the large, commanding features of the head of the **DEPARTMENT OF SECRET AFFAIRS** appeared.

'Ah!' announced Auntie Roz briskly. 'You're there. Jolly good. I suppose you want all the loose ends tying up, do you? Very well.'

Arabella shrugged. 'I'm more interested in the action than the boring talky stuff, to be honest. But go on, if you must.'

'Firstly,' said Auntie Roz, 'all the SIKBAG children have been safely returned, thanks to your clever spycraft, Flax. The disappearance is being explained by saying children were taking part in a massive game of hide-and-seek. People seem to be buying that, so far. Seems the public will swallow any old fib if you tell them it in a confident enough voice.'

Flax beamed with quiet pride.

'Secondly,' continued Auntie Roz, 'Miss April Spume and Master Sebastian Plum are being sent to the Archibald Honk School for Exceptionally Naughty Youngsters, where they will be studied by scientists, taught the error of their ways and soundly thrashed with a cricket bat.'

Dan gasped. 'Thrashed with a –?'

Auntie Roz guffawed. 'That last bit was my little joke. They shall of course be treated with the utmost kindness. Not that they deserve it, if you ask me. Now, watch this.'

The image of Auntie Roz vanished. In its place appeared four different video images showing gaping holes in the ground. With bursts of blue light, large buildings appeared in each of the four holes: the Bogey Cola bottling plant, the studios of Kidzland TV, the Snaztacular Ultrafun factory and, finally, the factory of Chimpwick's Chocolate.

'Once more, children are free to have their teeth rotted, their brains turned to mush and their attention distracted from schoolwork by all the pleasures of life – thanks to the Spy Toys.'

'Yeah, brilliant,' said Dan without interest. 'If that's everything, then, we'll say cheerio. Sorry to rush but I've booked us in for an intensive course of advanced spy training this afternoon and we don't want to be late. The worksheets look fascinating.'

'Ah,' said Flax. 'Sorry, Dan. Just remembered. Can't make the course because I promised Jack I'd pop round for a few games of **TURBO BADGER**. Dr Willows is joining us too. She's *so* good at that game. Well, you can't work *all* the time, you know.'

Arabella gave Flax a hard stare. 'You feeling OK, cottontail?'

'There is actually one small matter remaining,' said Auntie Roz with an odd grin.

The stomachs of all three toys knotted. Something told them trouble was coming.

'Do you remember,' asked Auntie Roz, 'a young lady by the name of Pandora Grebe whom I mentioned might be paying you a visit with a view to conducting an interview with you?'

'*Oh*,' said Dan.

'*Ah*,' said Arabella.

'*Er*,' said Flax.

'It seems she was found clinging to a discarded tyre floating in the middle of the Thames after being catapulted some considerable distance through the air. However, the young woman appears to have amnesia and cannot recall how this occurred. Ringing any bells?'

'Um,' said Dan.

'Umm,' said Arabella.

'Ummm,' said Flax.

Auntie Roz leaned in until her face filled the screen. 'Between you and me,' she whispered, 'I was never really that keen on the woman. Found her an awful bore, truth be told. So no harm done, eh, chaps? Good afternoon.'

The screen went blank.

HAVE YOU READ DAN, ARABELLA AND FLAX'S FIRST ADVENTURE?

Dan is a teddy bear.
He's made for hugging.
Aw, so cute, right?
WRONG!

Dan's so strong he can **CRUSH CARS**.
But what makes him a **FAULTY TOY**
could make him the **PERFECT SPY**.

Together with a robot police rabbit
and one seriously angry doll, Dan joins
a **TOP SECRET TEAM** designed to
STOP CRIMINALS in their tracks.

And just in time! An evil
elephant hybrid is planning to
kidnap the prime minister's son.

This is a job for...
SPY TOYS

SPY TOYS

PLAYTIME IS OVER

MARK POWERS

ILLUSTRATED BY
TIM WESSON

CHAPTER ONE

IF HUGS COULD KILL

It was a normal Tuesday morning at the factory of Snaztacular Ultrafun, the world's biggest toy manufacturer. Hundreds of conveyor belts whirred and clanked, carrying thousands of gleaming new toys towards the brightly coloured boxes in which they would be packed and delivered to shops. Balls, bikes, building blocks ... dolls, dominoes, ducks ... whistles, walkie-talkies, water pistols – the factory made them all.

Snaztacular Ultrafun's toys were not like the ones made by other companies. They were much cleverer and much more fun. Every toy contained a tiny computerised brain that gave it a personality and allowed it to walk and talk as if it were alive. They were the ultimate playthings: bikes that took you home if you were too tired to pedal, footballs who wanted to be kicked, board games whose pieces tidied themselves away once you had finished playing with them, dolls that acted just like real people. Children went crazy over them.

A red light flashed on a control panel. An alarm hooted.

'Yikes!' cried a white-coated technician who had been monitoring that morning's toy production, leaping out of his chair in surprise and banging his knee on the leg of his desk.

As each toy trundled on its way along the conveyor belt, it underwent a complicated series of scans and tests to make sure it was working properly. The company was rightly proud of its products and it wanted each toy to be perfect for the child who would eventually play with it. The red light meant a fault had been detected in one of the toys. And if the technician let a faulty toy leave the factory, he would get in big trouble with his boss.

Rubbing his knee, the technician examined his computer screen. The system had detected a problem with one of the Snugaliffic Cuddlestar teddy bears. The Snugaliffic Cuddlestar range were the most advanced teddy bears money could buy. They could sing lullabies, tell bedtime stories, bring you a glass of warm milk – but most of all they were designed for cuddling. When you hugged one of these bears, it actually hugged you back. In a world where many parents were simply too busy to do trivial things like hug their children, they sold in their millions.

The technician jabbed a button on his control panel. A huge metal claw descended from the ceiling and snatched the faulty teddy bear from the conveyor belt.

The teddy bear's eyes flickered open. He had been expecting to find himself in a cardboard box, rattling along the road in the back of a lorry on his way to a toyshop. Instead, he saw that he was in a dingy metal room. There was a table, a chair, a computer, a half-eaten ham sandwich. But no children to play with. He frowned. What was going on?

The door opened and the white-coated technician entered. He was carrying a large object that was hidden under a white sheet. He placed the object on the floor and consulted his computer screen.

'You are Snugaliffic Cuddlestar serial number 427935, yes? Made this morning?'

The teddy bear nodded. 'Yep.'

'It says here you've been assigned the name Dan. Is that correct?'

'That's me,' said the teddy bear. All Snaztacular Ultrafun toys were given individual names to help make them unique.

'Well, Dan, it's like this. The computer says you're faulty and it's up to me to find out whether it's something that can be fixed. We have a reputation for making the best toys in the world and we can't let shoddy merchandise out on to the market, can we?'

'Whatever you say, pal,' said Dan the teddy bear. He wasn't interested in boring stuff about markets or companies' reputations.

He was programmed for fun.

'Good,' said the technician. 'Let's get started.' He whipped the sheet off the mysterious object he had brought with him.

Dan's large brown eyes widened in surprise. The object appeared to be a little girl with a miserable expression and outstretched arms. She looked in serious need of a hug.

The technician rapped his knuckles on the girl's head. It made a hollow metallic sound. 'This is a hug test dummy,' he explained. 'The electronics inside it will tell us how good you are at hugging. Pressure, duration, snuggliness and so forth. Kindly hug the dummy for me, Dan.'

Dan dashed forward. This was more like it! He was made for hugging and now he had a chance to do some! He embraced the dummy girl in his furry arms and gave her a good squeeze.

There was a screech of wrenching metal followed by a loud bang. Dan stepped back, shocked. The dummy girl fell to the floor, her back bent horribly out of shape, her arms twisted at alarming angles and smoke pouring gently from her ears.

The technician raised his eyebrows. *'Oh dear.'*

'What happened?' asked Dan.

The technician waved a small electronic device over Dan's head. The device bleeped and the technician consulted a little screen set into it. 'Ah. Just as I thought. Unfortunate.'

'What is it?'

'You have a faulty snuggle chip. It's telling your robotic limbs to use a thousand times the usual pressure. In simple terms, you don't know your own strength. I'm afraid you can't be allowed near children.' He gestured to the twisted remains of the hug test dummy. 'Imagine if you did that to a real child. That would *not* be good for business.'

Dan shrugged. 'So reprogram me. Make me less strong.'

The technician shook his head. 'Much too fiddly to reprogram a single microchip. More trouble than it's worth, I'm afraid. Far easier to take you apart and start from scratch.'

'Take me *apart*?' Dan's robotic heart suddenly thumped with fear.

'Don't worry,' said the technician with a sickly smile. 'It won't hurt. Well, not much.' He pointed to a large yellow 'X' painted on the floor of the room. 'Kindly stand on the X for me, Dan, if you would.'

Dan shuffled over to the X. His furry brows

knitted in confusion. 'Why here?'

'Because that's where the trapdoor is.'

CHAPTER TWO

DOLL EAT DOLL

Dan found himself tumbling down a dark metal chute. He bumped and rattled against its sides for a short time until finally it spat him out on to a cold stone floor. He stood up, brushing the dust from his fur.

He was in an enormous darkened room. The floor was littered with old bits of cardboard, cogs, springs and broken pieces of electronic circuitry. Strange, indistinct shapes were moving all around him. The air was filled with a sickly mechanical humming sound.

'Hello?' he called nervously. This didn't

seem like a happy place. There were probably people around who could do with a nice big hug, he thought. Then he realised what might happen if he *did* hug someone. He shuddered. He would have to remember not to do any hugging if he could possibly help it.

A tall figure strode towards Dan out of the gloom. 'You! Identify yourself!' it barked. Dan jumped in alarm. The figure was a SuperTough Army Dude soldier toy, dressed in a smart uniform and carrying a toy rifle, his sturdy plastic body rippling with muscles. Dan could not help but notice that the soldier had no head. Instead, a large foot protruded from his neck.

'Erm, I'm Dan,' said Dan. 'Hi. I'm a Snugaliffic Cuddlestar.'

'Dan, sir! Pleased to meet you, sir!' announced the soldier brightly, facing slightly to the left of where Dan was standing and holding out his hand for him to shake.

Dan waved. 'I'm here. Can't you see me?'

The soldier shook its head (or rather the foot it had for a head) sadly. 'Apologies, sir! My eyesight is not 100 per cent effective due to a slight error during my manufacture. I have, as you may have noticed, a foot where my head should be.'

Dan reached out his paw and shook his hand but the soldier quickly snatched it away. 'Pleased to meet –'

'Yowch!' cried the soldier. 'You have quite the grip, sir! You nearly took my hand off!'

'Sorry,' said Dan. 'I'm too strong. That's

my problem. It's why I'm down here. I take it this is where they keep the faulty toys before they ... ?' His voice tailed away.

The soldier nodded its foot. 'Indeed, sir. But have no fear! You and I shall be out of here in no time!' He reached into his coat and produced a scroll of rolled-up paper tied with a blue ribbon. 'Here, sir, is a map showing the secret exit to this dungeon! And at long last I have met someone with good enough eyesight to read it for me! Observe!' He untied the ribbon and spread out the map on the dusty floor.

It was then that Dan saw that it wasn't a map at all, but an old chocolate bar wrapper.

'Well?' asked the soldier excitedly. 'Can you see the way out?'

'Erm,' said Dan awkwardly, 'not really, no.'

'Why not, sir?' demanded the soldier. 'The plastic duck I acquired it from assured me it was the very best map available. I exchanged my entire kitbag and spare batteries for it! Surely it must tell us *something* of the local geography?'

'I think you've been conned, pal,' said Dan.

A sudden booming growl filled the air, followed by the pounding of immense feet. Dan looked up, startled, and saw a huge shape advancing on them ...

'What did you say, sir?' yelled the soldier above the rising din.

'Never mind!' called Dan. 'Just run! Quick! Before it's too ...'

215

HAVE YOU READ DAN, ARABELLA AND
FLAX'S SECOND ADVENTURE?

WHO SAID YOU HAD TO
PLAY NICE?

The secret code that
controls every toy's mind
has been stolen!
It's up to the **SPY TOYS** – Dan, the
super strong teddy bear, Arabella, the
doll with a serious temper, and Flax, the
gadget-crazy robot rabbit to get it back
before toys everywhere turn BAD!

But who is the **EVIL MASTERMIND**
behind this plan? And can the
SPY TOYS stop them in time?

PLAY THE FREE
SPY TOYS GAME APP!

Download now from the iTunes App Store and Google Play Store.

And for more **SPY TOYS** action, check out **spytoysbooks.com**